Easter Parade

By Irving Berlin ✧ Illustrated by Lisa McCue

HarperCollinsPublishers

Never saw you look
Quite so pretty before;
Never saw you dressed
Quite so lovely, what's more,

I could hardly wait
  To keep our date
    This lovely Easter morning,
    And my heart beat fast
      As I came through the door,
      For . . .

In your Easter bonnet

With all the frills upon it

You'll be the grandest lady
In the Easter Parade.

I'll be all in clover

And when they look you over

I'll be the proudest fellow

In the Easter Parade.

On the Avenue, Fifth Avenue,

The photographers will snap us,

And you'll find that you're in the rotogravure.

Oh, I could write a sonnet

About your Easter bonnet

And of the girl I'm taking to
The Easter Parade.

Easter Parade

Words and Music by
IRVING BERLIN

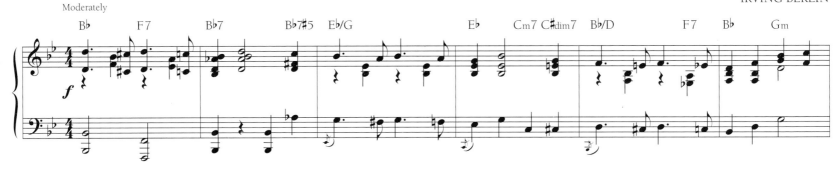

Nev-er saw you look Quite so pret-ty be - fore;_____ Nev-er saw you dressed Quite so love-ly, what's

Bb Cm/Bb Bb   Cm7 Eb/Bb F7/A   Bb   Eb/G   C7/E   C7   Eb/F F7   Bb/D   Gm

more,_____   I could hard-ly wait   To keep our date   This love-ly East-er   morn-ing,   And my heart beat   fast

C7/E   C7   F7   F7#5   Bb   F7   Bb7 Bb7#5   Eb/G   Eb   Cm7 C#dim7 Bb/D   F7

As I came through the door,   For... { (Boy:) In your } East-er bon-net With all the frills up-on it { You'll } be the grand-est
                                             { (Girl:) In my }   { I'll }

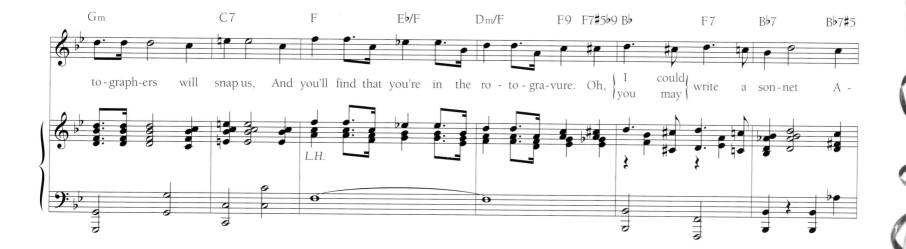

to-graph-ers will snap us, And you'll find that you're in the ro-to-gra-vure. Oh, { I could / you may } write a son-net A-

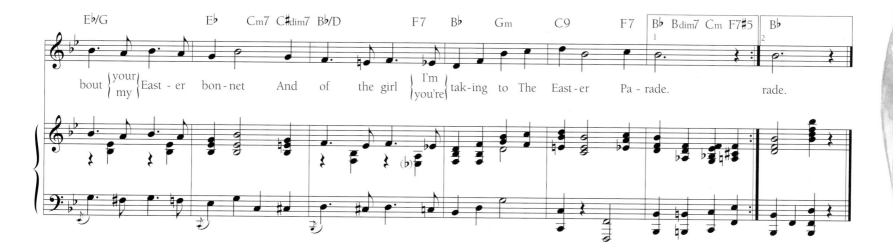

bout { your / my } East-er bon-net And of the girl { I'm / you're } tak-ing to The East-er Pa-rade. rade.

To Emma, who made a great little bunny
—L.M.

Easter Parade
Words and Music by Irving Berlin
© Copyright 1933 by Irving Berlin
© Copyright renewed 1960 by Irving Berlin
International Copyright Secured. All rights reserved.
Illustrations copyright © 2003 by Lisa McCue
Printed in the U.S.A. All rights reserved.
www.harperchildrens.com

Library of Congress Cataloging-in-Publication Data
Berlin, Irving, date
  Easter parade / by Irving Berlin ; illustrated by Lisa McCue.
    p.   cm.
  Summary: In an illustrated version of the song, a little bunny and her
father enjoy the Easter parade.
  ISBN 0-06-029125-7 — ISBN 0-06-029126-5 (lib. bdg.)
  1. Children's songs—United States—Texts.   [1. Songs.   2. Rabbits—
Songs and music. 3. Easter—songs and music.]   I. McCue, Lisa, ill.
II. Title.
PZ8.3.B4565 Eas 2003
782.42164'0268—dc21   2001024967
[E]   CIP
                                                                                 AC

Typography by Jeanne L. Hogle
10 9 8 7 6 5 4 3 2 1
❖
First Edition